Bootycandy

Robert O'Hara

A Samuel French Acting Edition

SAMUELFRENCH.COM
SAMUELFRENCH-LONDON.CO.UK

Cover Design by Bradford Louryk

ISBN 978-0-573-70398-0

www.SamuelFrench.com
www.SamuelFrench-London.co.uk

FOR PRODUCTION ENQUIRIES

UNITED STATES AND CANADA
Info@SamuelFrench.com
1-866-598-8449

UNITED KINGDOM AND EUROPE
Plays@SamuelFrench-London.co.uk
020-7255-4302

Each title is subject to availability from Samuel French, depending upon country of performance. Please be aware that *BOOTYCANDY* may not be licensed by Samuel French in your territory. Professional and amateur producers should contact the nearest Samuel French office or licensing partner to verify availability.

MUSIC USE NOTE

Licensees are solely responsible for obtaining formal written permission from copyright owners to use copyrighted music in the performance of this play and are strongly cautioned to do so. If no such permission is obtained by the licensee, then the licensee must use only original music that the licensee owns and controls. Licensees are solely responsible and liable for all music clearances and shall indemnify the copyright owners of the play(s) and their licensing agent, Samuel French, against any costs, expenses, losses and liabilities arising from the use of music by licensees. Please contact the appropriate music licensing authority in your territory for the rights to any incidental music.

IMPORTANT BILLING AND CREDIT REQUIREMENTS

If you have obtained performance rights to this title, please refer to your licensing agreement for important billing and credit requirements.

BOOTYCANDY was first produced by the Woolly Mammoth Theatre Company (Howard Shalwitz, Artistic Director; Jeffrey Herrmann, Managing Director) in Washington, D.C in June 2011. The performance was directed by Robert O'Hara, with sets by Tom Kamm, costumes by Kate Turner-Walker, lights by Colin K. Bills, and sound by Lindsay Jones. The Production Stage Manager was William E. Cruttenden III. The cast was as follows:

ACTOR ONE.................................Jessica Frances Dukes
ACTOR TWO.................................Phillip James Brannon
ACTOR THREE.................................Laiona Michelle
ACTOR FOUR.................................Lance Coadie Williams
ACTOR FIVE.................................Sean Meehan

BOOTYCANDY was subsequently produced by the Wilma Theatre Company (Blanka Zizka, Artistic Director) in Philadelphia, Pennsylvania in May 2013. The performance was directed by Robert O'Hara, with sets and costumes by Clint Ramos, lights by Drew Billiau, and sound by Lindsay Jones. The Production Stage Manager was Patreshettarlini Adams. The cast was as follows:

ACTOR ONE.................................Jocelyn Bioh
ACTOR TWO.................................Phillip James Brannon
ACTOR THREE.................................Benja Kay Thomas
ACTOR FOUR.................................Lance Coadie Williams
ACTOR FIVE.................................Ross Beschler

BOOTYCANDY received its New York premiere at Playwrights Horizons (Tim Sanford, Artistic Director) in August 2014. The performance was directed by Robert O'Hara, with sets and costumes by Clint Ramos, lights by Japhy Weideman, and sound by Lindsay Jones. The Production Stage Manager was Marisa Levy. The cast was as follows:

ACTOR ONE.................................Jessica Frances Dukes
ACTOR TWO.................................Phillip James Brannon
ACTOR THREE.................................Benja Kay Thomas
ACTOR FOUR.................................Lance Coadie Williams
ACTOR FIVE.................................Jesse Pennington

CHARACTERS

ACTOR ONE – Black Woman (age 20–30)

Plays: **YOUNG BLACK MOM, ADELLA, BIG SHIRLEY, WRITER 1, YOUNG SIBLING, INTIFADA**

ACTOR TWO – Black Man (age 20–30)

Plays: **SUTTER**

ACTOR THREE – Black Woman (age 30–40)

Plays: **EUDARRIE, LUCY, WRITER 2, MIDDLE AGED MOTHER, GENITALIA**

ACTOR FOUR – Black Man (age 30–40)

Plays: **REVEREND BENSON, WRITER 3, STEPFATHER, LARRY, OLD GRANNY**

ACTOR FIVE – White Male (age 20–40)

Plays: **ROY, CLINT, MODERATOR, OFFICIANT, WHITE MAN**

TIME

1970's – Present Day

SCENE BREAKDOWN

ACT ONE

Bootycandy

Dreamin' In Church

Genitalia

Drinks and Desire

Mug

Conference

ACT TWO

Happy Meal

Ceremony

Last Gay Play

Prison

iPhone

For my Mother, Lillie Garvin
and my Grandmother, Lizzie B. O'Hara

ACT ONE

Scene One. Bootycandy

(A **YOUNG BLACK MOM** *dresses her young son,* **SUTTER,** *who stands in his underwear, holding a children's dictionary.)*

SUTTER. Mommy where are we going?

YOUNG BLACK MOM. I'm going to the department store and then I'm taking you to the barber shop to get a haircut...

SUTTER. I don't want a haircut

YOUNG BLACK MOM. It's not about what you want... you need a hair cut...

SUTTER. Why do I have to get a haircut every time you say I gotta get a haircut?

YOUNG BLACK MOM. Because I'm the Mama. And you're the Son. Period.

SUTTER. Mommy what's a period?

YOUNG BLACK MOM. What you put at the end of a sentence why?

SUTTER. Because I had my ink pen burst in my pants the other day and the boys said that I had my period and I didn't understand what they meant *(whisper)* but mommy I think the period also means something else besides what you put at the end of a sentence.

(Silence.)

YOUNG BLACK MOM. Look it up...that's what I bought you that dictionary for.

SUTTER. I did look it up.

YOUNG BLACK MOM. And what did it say?

SUTTER. It said what you put at the end of a sentence.

YOUNG BLACK MOM. Well that's what I just said… did you remember to pull yourself back and wash?

SUTTER. Yes ma'am. Mommy why do I pull myself back and wash?

YOUNG BLACK MOM. Because you're not circumcised, Sutter.

SUTTER. Circus?!! We going to the CIRCUS!!!???

YOUNG BLACK MOM. Naw we ain't goin' to no damn Circus, calm down! You have to pull yourself back and wash because you have to keep your bootycandy clean.

SUTTER. Mommy why do you and granny call my dick bootycandy?

YOUNG BLACK MOM. It's not called a dick who told you that?

SUTTER. Nobody.

YOUNG BLACK MOM. It's called a bootycandy you too young to be calling it a dick don't let me hear you say that again have you lost your mind in real life?

SUTTER. But why do you and granny call it a bootycandy?

YOUNG BLACK MOM. I don't know I guess because its the Candy to the Booty!!

SUTTER. So can I lick it?

(Silence.)

YOUNG BLACK MOM. No.

SUTTER. Mommy what's a blowjob?

(Silence.)

YOUNG BLACK MOM. Look it up.

SUTTER. I did.

YOUNG BLACK MOM. And?

SUTTER. It wasn't in there.

YOUNG BLACK MOM. Then it must not be a word right, Sutter? So you should not say thangs that ain't words.

SUTTER. Well Alessa next door wrote me a letter and told me she wanted to give me a blowjob.

(Silence.)

YOUNG BLACK MOM. Alessa needs her ass beat... don't let me hear you say that no more.

SUTTER. Why?

YOUNG BLACK MOM. Because I said so and it ain't a word you looked it up didn't you and you didn't find it so I just told you that means it ain't a word so don't say it.

SUTTER. Mommy I still don't know why do I have to pull myself back and wash?

YOUNG BLACK MOM. I just told you because if you don't your bootycandy will get dirty down there.

SUTTER. Then what?

YOUNG BLACK MOM. Then you'll die from dirt and your dick'll fall off!!

(Silence.)

Where's your hat, Sutter?

SUTTER. In my coat pocket...

YOUNG BLACK MOM. Put it on your head

SUTTER. It's ugly.

YOUNG BLACK MOM. It's not ugly... it's cold outside... you wanna freeze to death and be hackin and coughin all night so that I'll have to be running you down to the hospital... who you tryin to be cute for... Alessa?... You can't be cute and warm too put that hat on your head boy that's what I bought it for.

*(**SUTTER** puts ugly hat on his head.)*

SUTTER. What store we going to first?

YOUNG BLACK MOM. Value City.

SUTTER. Goody they got that new Jackson Five tape recorder!!

YOUNG BLACK MOM. I don't want you to touch nothing you ain't fixin to buy… cuz why?

SUTTER. Cuz everything I touch turn to shit.

YOUNG BLACK MOM. Right.

SUTTER. When we get there I'm going to the toy department I won't touch nothin I promise.

YOUNG BLACK MOM. And when I come looking for you I want to be able to find you I don't wanna have to search that whole store all day for you I got too many things to do today… okay… you ready?

SUTTER. Yes ma'am.

YOUNG BLACK MOM. Give me your hand… and I hope I don't have tell you when we get into this store to please don't show your black ass… do I?

SUTTER. No ma'am.

YOUNG BLACK MOM. Because why?

SUTTER. Because if I show my black ass then that means you gonna have to show your black ass.

YOUNG BLACK MOM. And what?

SUTTER. Your black ass is bigger…

YOUNG BLACK MOM. That's right… let's go.

Scene Two. Dreamin In Church

(We discover **REVEREND BENSON** *behind a pulpit in an elaborate floor-length robe.)*

REVEREND BENSON.

church
the last time I spoke to you
we was talkin bout the I HEARD FOLK
and we agreed
that these I HEARD FOLK
loved to always come round us
whisperin
guess what
I HEARD

and we also agreed
that we had a lot of them I HEARD FOLK
ratt heah
in oura church

nah what I didn't tell you last time
was that these I HEARD FOLK
don't always
whispah
they sometimes write
and many of them have written me over the past few weeks
bout somethin that THEY HEARD
ya see when all the I HEARD FOLK get togetha on somethin
then it becomes
THEY HEARD
and thats what I wanna discuss today
church
WHAT
THEY HEARD

so somebody wake up Deacon Floyd and Sista Smith
somebody reach ova and tap Brotha Turner
and pinch Mother Carter and her three children

cos I'm liable to say somethin they don't wanna heah
I'm liable to put my foot down in somethin
that don't smell too fresh or feel just right
cos the THEY HEARD FOLK are fit
(as some might say)
FIT
TO BE READ

*(***REVEREND BENSON** *puts on reading glasses and reads a letter.)*

"Dear Rev. Benson
because you are in charge of oura house of Gawd
we feel that it is only ratt
that you know bout what is goin on
in oura church home"

"we know for a fact that there are a least
a half dozen"

"sexually
perverted"

"young men
who on a regular basis
sang Gawd's praises
in oura church choir"

"these young men have been seen
givin each otha knowin looks
holdin each othas hands
hangin round with certain"

"misfits"

"and

at times
kissin inside certain"

"bars"

"we realize that some of them
don't come from the best of families
some of them ain't even gat
a father round like they need
nor any type of a real motha fo that matter
but they must be put ratt
or gotten rid of
all togetha"

"cos Gawd don't llow no sin folk
in the kingdom
so we shouldn't llow that kind
in oura church"
"we know you will understand
Rev. Benson
and you will do the
Gawd-fearin
ratt thang
to do"

nah the THEY HEARD FOLK
almost never
sign they names
to nothin
and when they do
they sign
somethin lak
"anonymous"
or
"concerned worshipah"
or
"yo brotha in Gawd"

but this particular letter is signed

"the folks
who pay yo salary"

(**REVEREND BENSON** *folds the letter and takes his glasses off.*)

nah ya see church
RUMORS
git started
RUMORS
get goin
once the I HEARD FOLK
change into the THEY HEARD FOLK
and from this letter
I take it that
some folk
are concerned
that some of oura
choirboys
are a little
"freaky"
some folk
are worried
that some of oura
choirboys
are a little
"twisted"
cos they
at times
smile
at one anotha
cos they
at times
have a little
look see
at one anotha
What the Man say?

"You can't make no connection
With a screw
And another screw"

What he say?
"You need a Screw
And a
NUT!!!!!!!!"

So church
RUMORS
that's what these THEY HEARD FOLK do
RUMORS
that's how these THEY HEARD FOLK
function
but what you might not know church
is that some of these THEY HEARD FOLK
are tryin to start up new
RUMORS
round MY doorstep
peepin in my windows
tryin to see who I'm with
cos I ain't don took me no wife
some of these THEY HEARD FOLK lak to say
"Reverend!!!
when you gon get hitched"
some of these THEY HEARD FOLK
lak to say
"Rev!!!!"
"who you been seein"
"what you been doin"
"how you been doin it"
"when you been doin it"
"WHERE is yo' NUTT!!!!"

and I just wanna say
WHAT

I do
HOW
I do it

and the WHO WHERE and WHEN of it
that's MY bizness

Nah you see Church
This heah is one of dose
What what what what what what
What the woman on the TV say…
One of dose
Teachable Moments

How that ol' jingle jangle spiritual go
What it say?
"sometimes you feel like a Nut!"
And What?!!!
"sometimes you don't!"

I want you to have a look see
ratt nah
church
at what yo reverend IS
SIT UP!!!!!
and take a look see
at WHO yo reverend IS

(**REVEREND BENSON** *pulls up the hem of his robe and reveals he is wearing beautiful high heel shoes.)*

I got my heels on today church
my high heel shoes

(**REVEREND BENSON** *pulls out a glamorous wig from behind pulpit and places it on his head.)*

got my wig too, church
my special wig

(**REVEREND BENSON** *pulls out a purse from behind pulpit.)*

got my lipstick
got my rouge
and got my blush

Nah some of y'all bout to GET UP

I see some of y'all
gatherin ya thangs togetha
ready to run fo the hills
ready to fly outta my sight
but befo you
GET UP

let me tell you one mo thang
I'm tired
of creepin round

I'm tired
of sneakin round

I'm TIRED
watchin every which way I turn
lookin to see who lookin in my direction

I'm tired
of playin that game

I'm tired
of foolin with you all

I'm SICK
and I'm TIRED

nah some of y'all lookin at me
as if to say
well nah rev.
what you gon do nah?
nah that you don up and said it all
are you gon be a sissy nah
are you gon be a faggot nah
are you gon be a flamin queen nah
well I wanta let you know

yo words
cant TOUCH me
yo words
cant REACH me
I'm too HIGH nah
cos I gat the word of GAWD
deep down inside my soul
to protect me
and see me through ALLLL this mess
GAWD'S word is FIRE
SHUT UP IN MY BONES

so if you think I'm flamin nah
take a closer look see
cos I'm on FIIIIYAAAAHH

Yes Lawd
nah back to this letter
from the THEY HEARD FOLK
I just wanna say one thang
can I
can I park here fo a moment?
I'm gon park heah for ONE MOMENT
cuz if theres anybody in this heah church
that knows what JESUS
must've felt lak
back there in Galilee
its these heah
choirboys
ya see
they know
what it feels lak
to be
looked at
to be buked
and scorned
lak Jesus was

so befo ya start
recommendin
who should be put outta
this heah church
you oughta
check yo self
against my JESUS
you oughta
check yo self
against my GAWD

See y'all wanna go git yo quick fix
fo what ya see in THEM

(**REVEREND BENSON** *sing-speaks the rest.*)

(The spirit has reached him.)

But MY GAWD
MY, MY
MY, MY, MY
MY, MMY
MMY, MMY, MMY
MY, MY, MY
MY GAWD
WILL FIX YA UP RATT
and I wanna tell all you
CHOIRBOYS
up in heah

you ain't gotta be afraid
of who you are
you ain't gotta be afraid
of what you do

you ain't gatta be afraid!!!!!!

how ya walk
how ya talk
what ya wear
the curl in yo hair

you ain't gatta be afraid!!!!

how ya twirl
how ya whirl
and how ya swirl
cos the I HEARD FOLK
And the THEY HEARD FOLK
will always be sittin' around
speakin in tongues
signifi-in
stirrin up RUMORS
runnin from YOU
ta git they FIX
but you ain't gotta be afraid
of alllllll that MESS
Cos lak the lady with the money and the tv show say
THIS is a Teachable Moment
CHURCH

My GAWD tol me
say Rev. Benson
REVEREND
BENSON
Say You need to TELL ALLLL THE CHOIRBOYS up in heah
if ya feel lak SNAPPIN sometimes
up and down and round again
THAT'S ALLLRIGHT

if ya feel lak FLIPPIN yo wrist sometimes
as if ta say
"gon gurrlll gon"
THAT'S ALLLLRIGHT

I feel lak I might as well just let loose church
GOOD GAWD ALMIGHTY
if ya feel lak DRESSIN UP sometimes

(**REVEREND BENSON** *undoes his robe and reveals that he is wearing a divine dress.)*

THAT'S
ALLLLLLLLLLLLLLLLLLLLLLLLLLLLLL
RIGHT

cos lak the song says
in RUPAUL 19-93-72-24
SASHAY
SHANTE
SASHAY
SHANTE
SHANTE
SHANTE
TURN TO THE LEFT
TURN TO THE RIGHT
WERK
YOOOOOOOUUUUUU BETTA WERK!!!

SO FO ALL THE CHOIRBOYS UP IN HEAH
AND MORE THAN A FEW OF THE CHOIRGIRLS
TOO!!!!

SOMEBODY needs ta
STAND UP
and say "Rev. Benson
I'M WITH YA"
SOMEBODY needs ta
RIIIIIIIIIIISE UP
and say "Rev. Benson
WERK ON"
SOMEBODY needs ta
JUMP UP
and SAY "AAAAAAAMEN"
AMEN
AMEN
AMEN
AMEN

*(***REVEREND BENSON** *continues repeating "amen" for the rest of his life.)*

Scene Three. Genitalia
(A Phone [Land Line] Conversation)

EUDARRIE. How you gon go n name that chile Genitalia fool?

ADELLA. I ain't changin her last name ta no fool who tol you that?

EUDARRIE. I'm callin you a fool cuz you bout ta name that baby Genitalia, fool!

ADELLA. I like it it has a right nice ring to it.

EUDARRIE. Genitalia?!!

ADELLA. Yeah! Genitalia Lakeitha Shalama Abdul

EUDARRIE. That ain't no kinda name fo no chile soundin lak somethin you order to eat you don already put those other two you gat ta shame.

ADELLA. What about Avis and Cicada ain't nuthin wrong wit they names what you talkin?

EUDARRIE. One name afta a Rent-A-Car n otha name afta a blind insect.

ADELLA. So?

EUDARRIE. So yo name is Adella. How you git ta com up ta namin somebody geni –

(Beep.)

– hold on for a second gul let me see who this is on my otha line.

(Click.)

Hello?

BIG SHIRLEY. Gul have you heard what yo sista bout ta name that –

EUDARRIE. You know I did I'm talkin ta the heifa ratt nah.

BIG SHIRLEY. Well try n talk some sense inta her hell she might as well gon head and name it Vagina.

EUDARRIE. *(laughing)* Thas exactly what I was about to tell her but she don't wanna listen ta nobody n on top of that she gon tack on som shalaya shaluka muslim shit o somethin ain't nobody never heard of n you n me bof know she don't know a bit mo bout muslim than shit – chile hold on let me get her off the line –

BIG SHIRLEY. Tell her I say lay offa that pipe!

(Click.)

EUDARRIE. Adella you still there?

ADELLA. Yeah who dat on yo other line?

EUDARRIE. It's Big Shirley callin me cuz she heard you been consultin with Daffy Duck n the rest of the Looney Toon gang ova what ta name yo chile.

ADELLA. Y'all can say what ya won't but I lak the sound of it

EUDARRIE. And I like the sound of Fool, FOOL! let me gon and see what Shirley talkin bout you need ta take a lil time out n think about what it means to be puttin all that on a lil chile who dont know nuthin n can't tell you ta go ta hell fo namin it that, I'll call you in a bit you still goin ta the bingo?

ADELLA. I might try n git on ova there I was thinkin bout goin down ta the boat play me some quarter slots

EUDARRIE. Call me fo you leave…"Genitalia"…you a fool I see that nah…

(Click.)

Yeah Shirley gul I'm back

BIG SHIRLEY. You find out what she sniffin?

EUDARRIE. I don't know honey but it's strong whatsineva it is

BIG SHIRLEY. *(laugh)* Nah gul you never finish tellin me bout how she showed her ass out when y'all was bringin yo Aint Katie back from down Bama did Adella eva start the car back up, Eudarrie?

EUDARRIE. Naw! Not at first!! She gon tell me that she didn't have nough gas left to git me home and if I wasn't gonna split sista's money with her I could at least come up offa some money from my own pocket for a lil bit of gas.

BIG SHIRLEY. What?? Outta yo' own pocket??!!

EUDARRIE. That's when I looked ova and seen that the tank was reading half full, but she gon say that that means it's half empty, not half full.

BIG SHIRLEY. You know she pulled that same shit with me befo' when I had had her to take me to go git my carton of Virginia Slims menthols cross the river.

EUDARRIE. We five fucking blocks from my curbside and she tryin to give me some mess 'bout gas.

BIG SHIRLEY. She told me I owed her five dollars for taking me cross the gatdamn river –

EDUARRIE. All the time we racin down the street she screamin bout how I'm sittin on a whole heap of money I got from sellin' that ol piece of house of mine after Judge passed.

BIG SHIRLEY. I told her she can kiss the five dollar side of my ass crack…

EUDARRIE. Nah, I ain't git no helluva lot of nuthin for that house after it was all said and done.

BIG SHIRLEY. It ain't none of her bizness how much you gat.

EDUARRIE. It wasn't none of her bizness how much I gat from it in the first place.

BIG SHIRLEY. That's yo' money!!

EUDARRIE. It's my money!!

BIG SHIRLEY. Xactly.

EDUARRIE. That's xactly what I told her.

BIG SHIRLEY*. That's yo' money! And if you wanna take it and throw it up a wild hog's ass and yell SOOEY!!

EUDARRIE*. It's my money! And if I wanna take it and throw it up a wild hog's ass and yell SOOEY!!

BIG SHIRLEY. You Will!!

EUDARRIE. I Will!!

BIG SHIRLEY. Because it's Yo' Money!

EUDARRIE. Because it's My money! –

(Beep.)

BIG SHIRLEY. – hold on fo a second gul thats my otha line.

(Click.)

Hello?

LUCY. GUL SHE NAMIN HER CHILE PUSSY!!

BIG SHIRLEY. *(laughing)* Lucy you a fool she namin it Gentalia how you com up with PUSSY!

LUCY. Dats what I heard.

BIG SHIRLEY. Well you heard wrong, I'm talkin ta her sista Eudarrie ratt nah hold on.

(Click.)

(laughing)

Chile my sista Lucy on my other line so let me get off this phone you goin ta the bingo tonight o you gon try ta git ta the boat?

EUDARRIE. Adella talkin bout tryin ta go ta the boat but my number came through last night so I got me little bit of cash n I don't know if I wanna be losin it all on some slot machines so…ah don't know…but I'm sure I'll end up at one place o the otha…

BIG SHIRLEY. Give me a call fo you go I might join ya…

EUDARRIE. Alright chile, you take care, I talk ta you soon…

(Click.)

BIG SHIRLEY. Yeah gul, Genitalia…Genitalia somethin somethin muslim

LUCY. Lawd sweet Jesus. She don lost all of her mind!

Scene Four. Drinks and Desire

*(**SUTTER** and **ROY** at various bars throughout the city.)*

SUTTER. So what do you think?

(Silence.)

ROY. Sutter, I don't know.

SUTTER. Okay Roy.

ROY. I mean… I don't know when.
I know I
I would like to try.

SUTTER. Try what?

ROY. I don't know… something.

SUTTER. What?

ROY. I don't know Sutter.

SUTTER. What?!

ROY. I don't know
something!!

SUTTER. …when?

ROY. I.
do. not.
know.

SUTTER. Okay fine. Roy.

(Pause.)

ROY. …what would you want…
to do…
…huh?

(Silence.)

SUTTER. I would want…
to put your dick in my mouth
and suck on the tip of it gently
then lick the shaft
and maybe
maybe

kiss your balls
then deep throat you
...slowly... Roy.

(Silence.)

ROY. ...when?

SUTTER. Now.

ROY. We can't...do it here...

SUTTER. Let's go somewhere
your place

ROY. no

SUTTER. why not?
no ones there

ROY. I'd
I'd wanna be able to leave
if I didn't like

SUTTER. you'd like it

ROY....well I'd

SUTTER. you'd. like. it.

(Pause.)

SUTTER. You need more time?

ROY. No I
I actually don't need more time
I've thought about this a lot Sutter.

SUTTER. I know

ROY. An awful lot

SUTTER. I know

ROY. I thought about what if you were to

SUTTER. No

ROY. I know

SUTTER. No wigs

ROY. I know

(Pause.)

...would you let me fuck you?

SUTTER. Yes.

ROY. Without a condom

SUTTER. …maybe

ROY. Could I cum?

SUTTER. Where

ROY. Inside you

SUTTER. Where Roy.

ROY. …your mouth

SUTTER. Yes

ROY. Your ass

SUTTER. …no…
maybe…

(Pause.)

ROY. …okay

SUTTER. What?

ROY. Okay

SUTTER. What?!!

ROY. Let's go

SUTTER. Where?

ROY. Your place

SUTTER. Okay

ROY. Okay

SUTTER. Okay

ROY. Let's

SUTTER. Wait.

(Pause.)

ROY. What

SUTTER. What do you wanna do?

ROY. I tol you I don't

SUTTER. Say it

ROY. I don't really –

SUTTER. Say. It.

ROY. … I want you to ride my dick

SUTTER. Your dick

ROY. …my dick

SUTTER. Your big dick

ROY. I want you to ride my big dick
and let me fuck deep inside you
I wanna fuck your face
I wanna fuck your ass

SUTTER. Do you wanna fuck me?

ROY. …

SUTTER. Do you wanna fuck me?

ROY. Yes.

SUTTER. Will you suck my dick?

ROY. Yes.

SUTTER. Will you suck my nipples?

ROY. Yes

SUTTER. Will you eat out my ass?

ROY. Yes

SUTTER. And kiss me

ROY. No

(Pause.)

…let's go.

SUTTER. …let's go.

(Dark.)

(Then.)

(Light.)

ROY. I I
I've been uh
having thoughts

SUTTER. About what

ROY. You

SUTTER. …and?

ROY. …and other

SUTTER. What?

ROY. Men

(Pause.)

SUTTER. About me and other men or

ROY. Yes

SUTTER. Or you and other men

ROY. Yes

SUTTER. What?

ROY. About you and me
and other
men

SUTTER. …fucking

ROY. Yeah

SUTTER. You?

ROY. Yeah

SUTTER. About other men fucking you

ROY. Yeah

SUTTER. Okay

ROY. And you…
fucking me…

(Silence.)

SUTTER. I was 16

ROY. What?

SUTTER. My first time

ROY. Oh

SUTTER. You wanted to know didn't you

ROY. Yeah
…16?

SUTTER. Yeah

ROY. Did it hurt

SUTTER. Yeah

ROY. Pain

SUTTER. Pleasure…pain

pleasure…pain
pleasure…pain
pleasure

ROY. …who was

SUTTER. You want me to say my father

ROY. …no

SUTTER. You want me to say my uncle
Your uncle?

ROY. What?

SUTTER. It was your uncle

ROY. What?!

SUTTER. *(laugh)* Just kidding

ROY. *(laugh)* Okay

SUTTER. Actually it was your father.

(Silence.)

(Silence.)

I wanted

ROY. SHUT THE –

SUTTER. I wanted it
I asked for it
I begged for him to.

(Pause.)

You knew

(Pause.)

ROY. I didn't

SUTTER. …

ROY. I didn't know
for sure.

SUTTER. My sister knew
I told her

ROY. …when

SUTTER. The day you married her
And she said
She knew

ROY. …I'm sorry

*(**ROY** reaches out.)*

SUTTER. Don't touch
please

ROY. Okay

SUTTER. …thanks…

ROY. What?

SUTTER. Thank you.

(Silence.)

People
think
that we're together
here

ROY. I know

SUTTER. That doesn't bother you

ROY. Who gives a shit

SUTTER. That doesn't

ROY. No

SUTTER. You don't

ROY. No!

(Pause.)

I'm straight

(Pause.)

SUTTER. I know

(Dark.)

(Then.)

(Light.)

SUTTER. Please.

ROY. Okay.

SUTTER. Don't. Call. Anymore.

ROY. Okay

SUTTER. Don't. Write.

ROY. Okay

SUTTER. Anymore

ROY. Okay

SUTTER. You're straight

ROY. I know

SUTTER. Stay that way

(Silence.)

ROY. You tried once.
A girl.

SUTTER. Once.

ROY. Who

SUTTER. High school

ROY. Who?!

SUTTER. Nobody
you'd know

ROY. Who?!!

SUTTER. Tamara

ROY. Green?

SUTTER. Green.

ROY. No

SUTTER. Once.

ROY. And

SUTTER. Awful

ROY. …I tried

SUTTER. What?!

ROY. Tamara

SUTTER. Oh

ROY. Awful

(Laughter.)

SUTTER. Remember Kevin

ROY. Her brother

SUTTER. Yes

ROY. Nice

SUTTER. Ass

ROY. Yes!

(Pause.)

I mean –

SUTTER. Gym class

ROY. Every day

SUTTER. Every. Day.

ROY. Nice

SUTTER. Ass

(Silence.)

ROY. I wanna be your friend
just

SUTTER. Don't. Call.

ROY. Friends

SUTTER. Don't. Write.

ROY. …okay…

SUTTER. They need you

*(**ROY** reaches.)*

Don't.
Touch. Roy.

(Dark.)

(Then.)

(Light.)

ROY. If anybody found out

SUTTER. I know

ROY. Crazy

SUTTER. Yep…

ROY. Lose so much

SUTTER. Yeah

ROY. Definitely your sister

SUTTER. Yep.
Definite –

ROY. Why'd you come?

SUTTER. ...you called...

(Pause.)

ROY. I don't
I want you to know something

SUTTER. I know

ROY. You're not
the person
I wanna spend the rest of my life with
I can't make that type of
com –
com –
commitment

SUTTER. I know

ROY. Your sister
I love her

SUTTER. Ditto

ROY. We haven't touched since

SUTTER. You and my sister?

ROY. You and I.

SUTTER. Oh

ROY. We haven't touched since

SUTTER. That night

ROY. That
night.

(Pause.)

SUTTER. You wrote.

ROY. Yes

SUTTER. I asked you not to

ROY. I called
I wrote
I thought a lot... Sutter
was I good?

SUTTER. …no.

ROY. …no?

SUTTER. No
not as good desired

ROY. Oh

SUTTER. Desired
desire
was better

(Silence.)

ROY. I don't love you Sutter.

SUTTER. I know Roy.

ROY. I don't

SUTTER. Yeah

ROY. Really

SUTTER. I know

ROY. Desire

SUTTER. Yes

ROY. is better
…for us

SUTTER. …yes

(Pause.)

ROY. Stop it.

SUTTER. What

ROY. Stop it

SUTTER. I can't

ROY. Stop

SUTTER. What?!

ROY. Letting me
needing me
you make me feel
stop

(Pause.)

SUTTER. I don't love you
either
I never loved you

(Silence.)

ROY. …say it…

SUTTER. I never –

ROY. Don't lie

SUTTER. I didn't

ROY. Say it

SUTTER. No

ROY. Say it!

SUTTER. What?

ROY. SAY IT!!

SUTTER. I DON'T!

ROY. You love me Sutter.

SUTTER. No

ROY. Say it

SUTTER. …uh-uh…

ROY. Fuck you!!
Say it!!

SUTTER. Uh-uh

ROY. You do

SUTTER. Uh-uh

ROY. YOU DO!!!

(Pause.)

SUTTER. …

(crying)

…uh-uh …

(Pause.)

ROY. … I'm sorry

*(**ROY** reaches out.)*

SUTTER. Don't.
touch Roy.

ROY. I'm sorry

SUTTER. Please

ROY. I'm so –
okay

SUTTER. Thanks

ROY. What?

SUTTER. …thank you.

(Dark.)

(Then.)

(Light.)

*(***ROY** *alone.)*

(He waits.)

(He waits.)

(He waits.)

Scene Five. Mug

*(**CLINT** stands on the street…late at night…waiting for a bus… **CLINT** looks up and down the street…looks at watch…sighs… After a moment **CLINT** speaks to SOMEONE we can't see…)*

CLINT. …No

No.

No.

I said no…

Why would you want to do that?…

… I mean seriously…why would you want to do that?…am I rollin a Lexus here? …I'm waiting for the bus…it's 3am in the morning and I'm waiting for the bus because I only have three dollars and it costs that much just to sit down in a taxi at this time of the night

…look I got a driver's license metrocard and a few maxxed out credit cards…mints lint and 3 dollars… what are you gonna do with that? …you know what I'm saying? …don't you have better things to do besides bop me over the head and take my little cash that won't even buy you a beer at the bar down the street there… most certainly can't buy you any usable amount of drugs…

you would ruin my already bullshit of a night… and you'd ruin your life… because you'd have to kill me… thats the only way you'll take anything of mine…

and I'm certainly planning to either take you with me or take a large piece of you with me… so the cops would eventually find you… either here dead next to me or by doing some tests on whatever chunks of you I have between my dead fists or my dead teeth… they'd do DNA tests blood tests what have you tests and since you probably have a record already it won't take them long to find out who you are and where your mother lives because you obviously still live with her or maybe just maybe with your baby's mama and they'd track you down in a week maybe a month maybe a little later and they'd take you to court and whatever you don't confess to they'll prove to the jury you did it anyway… you'd go to jail for murder this time…a few other charges… end up back where you just got out of what 2 to 3 weeks ago?…

but this time that guy you fucked with when he first got there has now come up n gained weight been working out waiting for you to come back… he'll beat the living shit out of you and then stab a plastic man-made utensil in your eye or your neck or up your ass or maybe in that space from where I took that chunk of your flesh…wherever…

and you'd bleed to death thinking something like damn if I'd just left that muthafucka alone at that bus station late that one night I wouldn't be getting numb all over and going to hell right now as this asshole above me stomps my face into the concrete of this jail floor…

so…why don't you just go home…go to sleep…wake up…go down to…Mickey D's…the Gap…apply for a job…and…see what happens…

who knows…you might make enough to…I don't know – start payin child support on your what? Six kids? …even if you start giving support for one of them…that's a beginning…

treat your moms to a dinner out…a decent pair of "kicks" for yourself that you didn't have to "boost"… you might meet a few folks you'd never thought you'd ever hang out with…go out for a drink after work… shoot the shit…leave…and realize it's way later than you first thought but you got the last round at the bar with your new found non-delinquent friends so now you have just three dollars to your name…

you remember that you took your medication you bought that unlimited metrocard yesterday so you're cool...you wait for the bus... even tho it's late...too late for waiting...

then some kid'll come by you and...

...keep right on walkin...

because...he's got better things to do with his evening...he's just tryin to get home without getting jacked...himself...

(Silence.)

What's your name?

Anthony...I'm Clint.

...have a good night, Anthony...

...no...thank you...

*(**CLINT** looks at watch...)*

(and continues to wait for the bus...)

Scene Six. Conference

*(***SUTTER*** and a ***GROUP OF BLACK PLAYWRIGHTS****, all dressed in a variation of* **SUTTER***'s costume, and a white* **MODERATOR** *sit in a half circle facing the audience.)*

(Long silence.)

WRITER 1. …I'm sorry –

MODERATOR. Yes.

WRITER 1. I don't understand exactly

MODERATOR. What –

WRITER 1. Why we're here.

MODERATOR. Does anyone want to answer that for Kerry.

WRITER 1. Terry.

MODERATOR. For Terry.

WRITER 2. …I don't…understand either.

MODERATOR. So there are two of you who have absolutely no idea why you're here.

WRITER 3. Make that 3.

SUTTER. 4.

(Pause.)

MODERATOR. …None of you have any idea why we're here today?

(Silence.)

(embarrassed)

Well, someone screwed up didn't they? – Um…well…

WRITER 3. Is this like uh – group?

MODERATOR. A conference.

(Tension.)

WRITER 1. On what?

MODERATOR. Well…of course on…playwriting –

WRITER 2. Playwriting?

MODERATOR. Yes, you're all – is there a problem – you're all…playwrights –

WRITER 3. Is there a… Theme?

(The **MODERATOR** *looks at all of them in amazement.)*

MODERATOR. Are you serious?

WRITER 3. Do I look serious?

MODERATOR. Yes.

WRITER 2. What. Is the title of this conference –

MODERATOR. The title is… Black

SUTTER. Black??!!

MODERATOR. Fire

SUTTER. What??!!

MODERATOR. Hot –

WRITER 1. Hot?

MODERATOR. Emerging –

WRITER 3. I've been writing for 20 years.

MODERATOR. And Established –

WRITER 3. I haven't had a production in 20 years

MODERATOR. Unknown –

WRITER 2. I won a Pulitzer.

MODERATOR. *(genuine)*

You did, when?

(They look to him in amazement.)

I didn't – That's not in…my notes.

SUTTER. Who are you?

MODERATOR. I'm the Moderator.

(Pause.)

WRITER 1. Is this a Break Out Session?

MODERATOR. No.

WRITER 2. So we're the conference? The entire conference?

MODERATOR. Well obviously there's an audience.

(He motions to the live audience and they look at the live audience as if they are seeing them for the first time.)

(Silence.)

WRITER 3. *(serious)*
What the fuck is going on?

MODERATOR. *(to live audience)*
Ladies and gentlemen there's been a slight misunder –

SUTTER. Is this a Talkback –

MODERATOR. No it's a conference. You all signed a release form –

WRITER 1. Release from what?!!

MODERATOR. A Release form not a re – You were – I'm sorry someone screwed up. This is the part of the conference where we ask you what...you're working on. Then we have a Q and A

WRITER 2. About what?

MODERATOR. Your work.

WRITER 3. Why?

MODERATOR. Because that's part – this is the part of the conference where that happens – where that is done... People talk about – a little about what you're – then

(Silence.)

So what are you all working on, Kerry – uh Terry – O'Malley, by the way I've often wondered, how exactly did you get the name Terry O'Malley – seems odd for a black playwright to have the last name O'Malley how did that come about?

WRITER 1. Slavery.

(Silence.)

MODERATOR. Ok...um... So what are you working on?

WRITER 1. I'm working on a play about a Preacher...who comes out of the closet...

MODERATOR. Ok

WRITER 1. In front of his Congregation...

MODERATOR. Ok...

WRITER 1. In a dress...

MODERATOR. Ohhhkay... Well...you don't actually think anyone's going to produce that play do you?

WRITER 1. No.

MODERATOR. Good. Um…

(turns to **WRITER 2***)*

And you?

WRITER 2. You don't even know my name do you?

MODERATOR. My-ke-le

WRITER 2. Michael.

MODERATOR. Michael. Strange name for a woman.

(Silence.)

Right. What are you working on?

WRITER 2. I'm writing a play about a woman on the phone. With some other women. Talking about pussy.

MODERATOR. What does that have to do with Race?

WRITER 2. What does pussy have to do with Race?

MODERATOR. What do women on the phone talking about pussy have to do with Race?

WRITER 2. Why does it have to have anything to do with Race?

MODERATOR. You're a black playwright.

WRITER 2. Yeah.

MODERATOR. And you're just writing a play about a woman on the phone with other women?

WRITER 2. Yeah. And pussy.

MODERATOR. And it has nothing to do with Race?

WRITER 2. …No.

MODERATOR. Ok.

(turns to **WRITER 3***)*

So um… I see here that you've changed your name to a Symbol.

WRITER 3. Yes, I felt that my parents had given me a European oppressor's name.

MODERATOR. So now you write as just a Symbol.

WRITER 3. Yes.

MODERATOR. And what does your symbol symbolize?

WRITER 3. What do you think?

MODERATOR. *(looks at paper)*

Well…to me…it looks like…

(examines the paper seriously)

Two people fucking?

WRITER 3. Exactly.

MODERATOR. Ok. What are you working on?

WRITER 3. I'm working on a play about two people fucking… A man and his Brother… In law.

MODERATOR. In a symbolic way.

WRITER 3. No they really fuck each other.

MODERATOR. Oh.

WRITER 3. In the Butt.

(Silence.)

They're also best friends.

MODERATOR. Ohhhh… Okay…now I get it…that's really an insightful idea for a play. Great…

(to **SUTTER.***)*

Now Sutter, you've actually had a play done just recently…right here on this very stage as a matter of fact.

SUTTER. Yes.

MODERATOR. I saw it…the title is slipping my mind, but… what was it called?

SUTTER. *Mug*

MODERATOR. *Mug*…yes! And when was it done?

SUTTER. Ten minutes ago.

MODERATOR. Right… Ok. Now that play was about a White Man –

SUTTER. It wasn't about a white man –

MODERATOR. It wasn't?

SUTTER. No. It had nothing to do with a white man.

MODERATOR. But… I recall a white man being on the stage…for the entire play.

SUTTER. So.

MODERATOR. There were no other people on stage with him.

SUTTER. So.

MODERATOR. So your play *Mug,* which only has a White Man on stage by himself the entire –

SUTTER. How do you know he was white?

MODERATOR. He wasn't white?

SUTTER. He was a white actor.

MODERATOR. But he wasn't playing a white character?

SUTTER. I'm just saying my play is not about a white man… it's about avoiding a Mugging…the play could've been done with a blue midget…

(Pause.)

MODERATOR. So the white actor was actually playing a Blue Midget and not a white man?

SUTTER. It has nothing to do with a white man. I don't write plays about white people.

MODERATOR. Right…right… So what are you working on now?

SUTTER. I'm doing rewrites on a piece about how my mother use to call my penis Booty Candy.

MODERATOR. *(serious)*

… Did she know you were gay when she called it that?

SUTTER. … What?

(looks to the audience)

MODERATOR. Booty. Candy. Did she know you were…

(He makes a gay gesture. Looks to the audience. Then back to **SUTTER.***)*

…nothing.

(Silence.)

WRITER 3. Is there a Stipend for this conf –

MODERATOR. It's in your pocket – packet – it should've- it's in the packet that you got – you'll get –

WRITER 1. What is this conference about –

MODERATOR. This conference has been convened to open up the question of the debate that has been the contention of the controversy inside the dialectic surrounding the conundrum while we investigate and raise query into the interrogation on the state of African – American –

WRITER 1. What the fuck are YOU talking about?!!

MODERATOR. The question.

WRITER 2. There's something seriously wrong with you.

MODERATOR. Is that a question?

WRITER 3. *(pointing to audience)*

Are those subscribers?!

MODERATOR. *(looking out at the audience)*

...Not for long.

(back to **WRITERS***)*

So... Each of you seem to have a strong facility with language and structure as well as grappling with some rather provocative issues and risky situations... I'm wondering what you are hoping the audience comes away with after seeing your work?

SUTTER. I think the Audience should Choke.

MODERATOR. Choke?

SUTTER. Asphyxiate.

MODERATOR. To death?

WRITER 1. I don't want them to digest it easily.

WRITER 2. It wasn't easy to write it and it shouldn't be easy to experience it.

WRITER 3. Exactly. It should not melt in yo' mouth.

SUTTER. The work should be work.

WRITER 1. After you choke on something and you struggle to get it down your throat. You can FEEL its presence in the space it went through.

WRITER 2. It lingers there.

WRITER 3. There is a physical memory after one chokes.

WRITER 2. Lingering

SUTTER. It makes you aware that all chocolate cake…ain't the same.

WRITER 1. Some of 'em gats Nutz in 'em.

WRITER 2. Some of 'em filled with cream.

WRITERS 3. Others topped with Cherries.

MODERATOR. Are we talking Auto Erotic Asphyxiation?

WRITERS. Yes.

MODERATOR. Or Choking on a big piece of Fried Chicken Neck Bone.

WRITERS. Yes!!

(The light and sound changes.)

(The **WRITERS** *and* **SUTTER** *begin to chant:)*

WRITERS AND SUTTER.

Choke Muthafucka Choke!
Choke Muthafucka Choke!
Choke Muthafucka!
Choke Muthafucka!
Choke Muthafucka Choke!

(Lights and sound change back to normal and we are back at the conference in front of the gathered audience.)

(The **MODERATOR** *begins to choke.)*

WRITERS AND SUTTER. Breathe.

(He manages to breathe. The **MODERATOR** *looks out.)*

MODERATOR. Let's all take a short… Breather.

(Intermission.)

ACT TWO

Scene Seven. Happy Meal

(Seated at the kitchen table.)

(A Happy Meal dinner has been eaten.)

(A **YOUNG SIBLING** *plays with an action figure from a Happy Meal. A* **STEPFATHER** *looks at horse racing stats in the paper. A teenage son,* **SUTTER**, *reads a Jackie Collins novel. A* **MIDDLE AGED MOTHER** *talks to no one in particular.)*

MIDDLE AGED MOTHER. …You know Barbara sits up there at that front desk and thinks she's runnin shit but she ain't… She sits there all damn day being nosey, in and out of other folk's bizness and thinks she's the head nigga in charge but I had to tell her fat ass today that she wasn't runnin shit… She likes to sit up there and run her damn mouth all damn day with her nosey ass…and like I said, I walked right up to her today and had to put her in her place… I had to just let her know, you know, that she wasn't running shit… She sit right up there, jabbering on that damn phone for half a damn hour, looking like she's in charge of something but I walked right up to her this morning and said "Barbara, you ain't runnin shit around here"… I told her, I said, "Barbara, you need to know something and I'm gonna be the one to tell you"… I looked her right in the face when I got in today and saw her sitting up there with her chest poked out with that damn raggedy ass blue sweater she likes to hang across the back her damn chair…and I said "Barbara, there is something that needs to be said so I'm gonna be the one to say it"… I went right into work this morning and saw her sitting there and marched my fat ass right up into her face and said "Barbara – "

TEENAGE SUTTER. A man followed me home today.

MIDDLE AGED MOTHER. " – you ain't the one running shit around – "

(to **TEENAGE SUTTER***)*

What?

TEENAGE SUTTER. A man tried to follow me home today.

MIDDLE AGED MOTHER. What are you talking about?

TEENAGE SUTTER. A man –

MIDDLE AGED MOTHER. What man?

TEENAGE SUTTER. I don't know his name.

(Silence.)

MIDDLE AGED MOTHER. What was you doing?

TEENAGE SUTTER. …Nothing.

MIDDLE AGED MOTHER. You had to be doing something for some man to try and follow you home. Ain't no man ever tried to follow me home.

TEENAGE SUTTER. I was at the library.

MIDDLE AGED MOTHER. Doing what?

TEENAGE SUTTER. …Reading.

MIDDLE AGED MOTHER. Reading what?

TEENAGE SUTTER. A Book.

MIDDLE AGED MOTHER. You was just sitting up in a Library reading a Book and some man got up and decided to try to follow you home.

TEENAGE SUTTER. Yes ma'am.

MIDDLE AGED MOTHER. He didn't say nothing.

TEENAGE SUTTER. No ma'am.

MIDDLE AGED MOTHER. He just started following you home.

TEENAGE SUTTER. Yes ma'am.

MIDDLE AGED MOTHER. …Well you had to have done something for him to start following you home.

Folks don't just up and start following teenage boys home just for no reason. You had to have been doing something to –

TEENAGE SUTTER. I was reading a Book in the Library. I left the library and he started following me. I went down the wrong street to trick him. Then… I ran.

MIDDLE AGED MOTHER. Iran?… What Iran got to do with it? Who you know in Iran?

TEENAGE SUTTER. I Ran… through someone's back yard… I got to our street and I think I lost him but I know he was trying to follow me home.

(Silence.)

(The **MIDDLE AGED MOTHER** *looks to the* **STEPFATHER.***)*

STEPFATHER. *(simple fact)*

You need to take up some Sports.

TEENAGE SUTTER. Sports?

STEPFATHER. Wrestlin.

TEENAGE SUTTER. Wrestling.

STEPFATHER. Yeah. Football, wrestlin, something. You need to start doing some sports. You come to this table every night with a book in your hand.

TEENAGE SUTTER. …A MAN. Followed me home today –

STEPFATHER. Baseball –

TEENAGE SUTTER. And it wasn't the first time.

(Silence.)

(The **MIDDLE AGED MOTHER** *looks to the* **STEPFATHER.***)*

MIDDLE AGED MOTHER. *(to* **TEENAGE SUTTER***)*

…How many times has this man tried to follow you home?

TEENAGE SUTTER. A few times.

MIDDLE AGED MOTHER. A few times.

TEENAGE SUTTER. After he put his arms around me…while I was waiting for the bus… In front of the school. He sometimes comes to the front of the school and waits for me with the other kids and…one day he came over to me and asked me if I was lonely. I said…yes. He said that I didn't have to be lonely. He said he had two sons and when they get lonely he hugs them. So he asked me if I needed a hug and I said…yes. And he put his arms around me and asked me if I wanted to come back to his place…

(Silence.)

(The **MIDDLE AGED MOTHER** *looks to the* **STEPFATHER.***)*

STEPFATHER. Kung fu.

(Silence.)

TEENAGE SUTTER. …He would wait for me after the bus brought us back from King's Island. When I was working there over the summer. Remember? I called you and said I wanted you to come pick me up? I said there was a man who always waited for me after the bus left us off at night. And you said to bring my ass home and quit talking silly. That's the same man.

(Silence.)

MIDDLE AGED MOTHER. This school year. No musicals.

TEENAGE SUTTER. But they're doing *The Wiz.*

MIDDLE AGED MOTHER. You are not going to be in no damn *Wiz.*

TEENAGE SUTTER. I've been cast as the Scarecrow already.

MIDDLE AGED MOTHER. I don't care if you been cast as the Scarecrow's Mama. You are going to walk in there and tell that teacher that you can't do no more musicals because you have to go wrestle…or bounce a ball…or jump a hurdle.

TEENAGE SUTTER. Michael Jackson played the Scarecrow.

MIDDLE AGED MOTHER. I dont care if Michael Jackson's Mama played the Scarecrow!

STEPFATHER. *(simple fact)* You need to start bending your knees when you pick stuff up.

(Silence.)

TEENAGE SUTTER. What?

MIDDLE AGED MOTHER. You don't say "what" to him. This is your father.

TEENAGE SUTTER. Step father.

MIDDLE AGED MOTHER. What??

TEENAGE SUTTER. Nuthin.

STEPFATHER. You need to start bending your knees when you pick stuff up…and when you empty your plate in the garbage.

TEENAGE SUTTER. Uh… Okay.

MIDDLE AGED MOTHER. Okay???

TEENAGE SUTTER. *(to* **STEPFATHER***)*

Yes sir.

STEPFATHER. And you need to stop playing those Whitney Houston albums… And stop talking on the phone for three hours every night with Brandon about *Star Search.* And start mowing the lawn twice a week.

MIDDLE AGED MOTHER. And wash my car.

STEPFATHER. And scrub the bathroom with more Comet.

MIDDLE AGED MOTHER. And do the dishes without listening to that Culture Club.

STEPFATHER. And take them stickers of DeBarage and Madonna and Prince and the Jacksons off the side of your bunk bed.

MIDDLE AGED MOTHER. And stop watching *Entertainment Tonight.*

STEPFATHER. And stop playing so much UNO.

MIDDLE AGED MOTHER. And ride your bike around the corner a few times everyday.

STEPFATHER. And put that Train set together downstairs.

MIDDLE AGED MOTHER. And stop pretending to Conduct a Gospel Choir in your room with the door closed.

STEPFATHER. And stop making up Songs about Food.

MIDDLE AGED MOTHER. And stop taking your little sister out of her top bunk to sleep in your bottom bunk with you every night because you're scared of the dark and then putting her back in her top bunk before we come in and wake you up for school.

STEPFATHER. And stop sitting down to Pee.

MIDDLE AGED MOTHER. And build a Snowman for once in your life.

STEPFATHER. And stop playing with my Anal Beads.

MIDDLE AGED MOTHER. And learn how to float.

STEPFATHER. And stop jiggling so much when you walk.

MIDDLE AGED MOTHER. And Track some dirt in this house from playing in some field.

STEPFATHER. And learn the difference between a wrench and pliers.

MIDDLE AGED MOTHER. And stop snapping your bubble gum.

STEPFATHER. And build a Tree House out back.

MIDDLE AGED MOTHER. And feed and walk that Dog.

(Silence.)

TEENAGE SUTTER. There are no Trees out back and the dog died last year.

MIDDLE AGED MOTHER. Are you giving us word for word?

TEENAGE SUTTER. I don't understand what any of this has to do with what I just said.

MIDDLE AGED MOTHER. What about it don't you understand?

TEENAGE SUTTER. A man followed me home. And you're asking me what did I do??? You're telling me to start wrestling and stop doing musicals and –

MIDDLE AGED MOTHER. What is that book you're reading?

(She takes the book.)

TEENAGE SUTTER. ... Jackie Collins' new book.

MIDDLE AGED MOTHER. Where did you get THIS?

TEENAGE SUTTER. The Library.

MIDDLE AGED MOTHER. Don't this book got a lot of fuckin in it.

TEENAGE SUTTER. *(duh)*

It's Jackie Collins.

MIDDLE AGED MOTHER. *(flipping pages)*

Barbara has been sitting up there at that front desk all damn week reading this same damn book, I knew it looked similah. She been sittin up there talking about it on that damn phone and all I could hear coming out her damn mouth was about how somebody fucked somebody else. From what Barbara be talking this book is ALL about Nuthin but Fuckin. And you mean to tell me that you have been sitting here night after night at my dinner table reading books about Fuckin!

TEENAGE SUTTER. I read Stephen King too.

STEPFATHER. Ain't his books about Killing folks?

TEENAGE SUTTER. Not exactly –

MIDDLE AGED MOTHER. Have you lost your mind in real life?

TEENAGE SUTTER. No ma'am.

MIDDLE AGED MOTHER. I go to work everyday to put clothes on your back and Happy Meals in your mouth and you come to this table reading books about killing and fuckin... THAT'S why that damn man from Iran was following you home. If every time he sees you, you sitting up somewhere reading about killing and fuckin it must mean you want to be kilt and then fucked.

(Silence.)

TEENAGE SUTTER. I finished all the Encyclopaedia Browns that they have in the library so I just started reading –

MIDDLE AGED MOTHER. Encyclopedia who???

TEENAGE SUTTER. Brown.

MIDDLE AGED MOTHER. What Brown got to do with it? I'm sitting here trying to figure out how to stop you from gettin raped up the ass and you talking about

Colors.... You need to Grow. Up... You are getting too old to be sitting up in here Reading all damn day.

STEPFATHER. Calm down honey.

MIDDLE AGED MOTHER. No. This is a conversation that needs to be had and if you're not going to have it, cuz you ain't his Real damn Daddy, then I guess I will have to have it.

(to **TEENAGE SUTTER***)*

I knew there was going to be troubles with you. Your Grandmama told me that I shouldn't be making you wash dishes and do laundry but I told her to mind her own damn bizness cuz you was my chile. But I knew from the moment you walked in here when you was little asking me about Periods and Blowjobs that you was going to bring me the troubles. You the only little boy that would come asking his mama why his dick was crooked and why his pee came out to the left side.

STEPFATHER. It's okay, honey.

MIDDLE AGED MOTHER. Booty Candies! Thats what he was concerned about when he was little and now I see that I should have never given you that damn Dictionary because now all you is interested in is Reading some ol Nasty Shit. How on earth do you expect to get a Woman when you grow up if all you know how to do is Read...and Clap...and Do Musicals?... You will NOT be going to Show Choir Camp THIS Summer you can forget about That!

TEENAGE SUTTER. But Mom!!!

MIDDLE AGED MOTHER. Don't But Mom Me! This summer you will learn to CATCH. SOMETHIN!... I don't give a damn what kind of ball it is but you will spend this coming summer with BALLS in yo FACE!!!

(Silence.)

Period.

(She gets up from the table and leaves, taking the Jackie Collins book.)

(Silence.)

*(***STEPFATHER*** sits for an awkward moment. He tries to say something but he is just…awkward.)*

(He gets up and leaves.)

*(***TEENAGE SUTTER*** looks over at ***YOUNG SIBLING*** who has been sitting playing with a Happy Meal toy this entire time.)*

(Silence.)

TEENAGE SUTTER. *(quiet)*
Call… Granny.

YOUNG SIBLING. For what?

TEENAGE SUTTER. Ask her if we can come over this weekend.

YOUNG SIBLING. Why cain't you axe her yourself?

TEENAGE SUTTER. I'm too old to be asking if I can come over.

(Beat.)

YOUNG SIBLING. What the fuck do I get if I axe her.

TEENAGE SUTTER. …I'll teach you that new dance Michael Jackson do.

YOUNG SIBLING. …Promise.

TEENAGE SUTTER. Promise.

(Beat.)

*(***YOUNG SIBLING*** gets up and leaves with toys.)*

(Silence.)

*(***TEENAGE SUTTER*** sits a moment.)*

(Then.)

(He retrieves a hidden Stephen King paperback.)

(He opens his book and reads.)

Scene Eight. Ceremony

(An **OFFICIANT** *stands in front of an audience at this ceremony.)*

OFFICIANT. Dearly Beloved. Today is the beginning of a bold new step to clarity and fulfillment. You have been asked here to bear Witness. Witness to a profound and sacred ceremony that stands in the face of homophobia and all prejudice. Witness to two individuals who not just five years ago requested your presence in this exact same tropical destination for what they believed then would be an everlasting celebration of their love and…commitment. You come here Today to share a moment of Non-Commitment. Therefore, on behalf of Genitalia and Intifada. Welcome.

(Two obvious **LESBIANS** *enter.)*

Today we come to encourage, celebrate and support the covenant these two people, Genitalia and Intifada, beloved to us, now make, and to share in the joy that Genitalia and Intifada are feeling as they pledge their Non-Commitment to each other. We rejoice and celebrate in the ways life has led them to each other and gotten them to the place where they now stand.

(to **GENITALIA***)*

Genitalia, the woman who stands here is going to be your Ex-Partner. She will no longer look to you for comfort, for support, for love, for understanding, for encouragement, nor for protection. You may now take her for granted, and never have to stand by her for good or ill.

GENITALIA. *(to* **INTIFADA***)*

Intifada… Today. In the presence of God and family and friends, I sever my life from yours. Wherever you go, I will not be there. Whatever you face, you will face without me.

OFFICIANT. Intifada. What I said to her. Consider me having said it to you.

INTIFADA. *(to* **GENITALIA***)*
Genitalia, what you have said to me, I now say back to you and would like to add that you Fuck Yourself.

OFFICIANT. And Now a Passage will be read by Reverend Benson.

*(***REVEREND BENSON** *appears.)*

REVEREND BENSON. In the Bible, Cicely Tyson wrote, so beautifully about the power of hatred in her first Book of Letters to the Hobbits:

"Get your own Milk and Sugar, muthafucka."

"I Speak in tongues of men and devils, but have not love, I am nosey and vindictive and funky."

"And if I have prophetic powers, and understand all mysteries and all knowledge, and if I have all faith, so as to remove the mountains of bullshit, but have not love, then fuck it, I will have not love."

"Hatred bares all things, believes all things, hopes all things, endures all things."

"When I was a child, I spoke like a child, I thought like a child, I reasoned like a child, when I became a man, I went on the internet, and spoke like a child, and thought like a child, and reasoned like a child."

"So faith, hope, hatred abide, these three; but the greatest of these is Hatred."

"Get your own Milk and Sugar…muthafucka."

*(***REVEREND BENSON** *exits.)*

(Beat.)

*(***GENITALIA** *takes out a piece of folded colorful paper and begins to read.)*

GENITALIA. "I, Genitalia, named so by my Mother, Adella Missatoof, a trailblazer before her time, who decided that her daughter should know that with a Beautiful name comes many haters. I affirm my hatred for you, Intifada, as I invite you to die a slow painful death from this very moment. You are the most ugly, stupid, self centered person I have ever known. With unkindness, selfishness, and cynicism, I will work against your side to create a living hell for you. I evict you, Intifada, from my condo, to no longer have and no longer hold, from this day forward, for my better and your worse, for my richer and your poorer, in your sickness and my health, for as long as I shall live and you shall suffer."

*(**INTIFADA** takes out a piece of folded colorful paper and begins to read.)*

INTIFADA. "Genitalia, your Mama was a Fool and a Ho. Your name attached to your face, means Stank Pussy. And I, Intifada, from the moment I first saw you, knew you were the one who would steal my money. Your cancerous heart, and your brain tumor inspired me to treat you like the cunt you revealed yourself to be. I promise to hate you for eternity, disrespecting you, dishonoring you, being as unfaithful to you now as I have been throughout our whole disgusting relationship. This is my solemn vowel."

(Silence.)

*(**GENITALIA** takes out another piece of folded colorful paper and begins to read.)*

GENITALIA. "Intifada, today I become your Ex and you become my Ex-Lax. I shit you out of my life. I promise to keep myself closed off from you, and never again let you into my innermost fears or feelings, secrets or dreams. I promise to grow old without you, to be unwilling to face change as we both change, keeping our relationship dead and cold."

(Silence.)

*(**INTIFADA** takes out another piece of colorful folded paper and begins to read.)*

INTIFADA. "Genitalia, today I become your Ex-Lax… And hope you are constipated."

OFFICIANT. Since it is your intention to be Non-Committed, join your fists and declare your consent.

*(**GENITALIA** and **INTIFADA** fist bump.)*

Genitalia, Do you take Intifada to be your unlawfully Non-Committed Ex as long as you both shall live?

GENITALIA. I Do.

OFFICIANT. Intifada, do you take Genitalia for the unlawfully Non-committed Ex stuff I just said?

INTIFADA. I Don't.

(Silence.)

OFFICIANT. Excuse me?

INTIFADA. *(to **GENITALIA**)*

I love you… let's work it out… I need you…

GENITALIA. Intifada –

INTIFADA. Genitalia, I love you. I want to grow old with you. Let's give us another chance. Please.

(Silence.)

*(**GENITALIA** looks to the gathered audience.)*

*(Then back to **INTIFADA.**)*

Please baby.

GENITALIA. …Ok.

INTIFADA. Sike!! You stupid DYKE. I hate your fucking guts and don't want to see you again until they're carving up your fucking tumor for science.

*(to **OFFICIANT**)*

My answer is I Do.

OFFICIANT. The Ceremonial Rings symbolize unity, a circle unbroken, without beginning or end. And today, Genitalia and Intifada take back their rings, as a confirmation of their vows to Non-Commit, to work at all times to create a life that is incomplete and broken, to never love each other again. May the Lord bless these rings which you take from each other as a symbol of your hatred and infidelity.

(to **GENITALIA.***)*

Take her hand, and state your pledge to her, repeating after me.

*(***GENITALIA** *takes* **INTIFADA***'s hand in her own.)*

With this ring I Non-Commit.

GENITALIA. With this ring I Non-Commit.

OFFICIANT. I remove my hand and heart as I know they will be unsafe with you.

GENITALIA. I remove my hand and heart as I know they will be unsafe with you.

OFFICIANT. All that I am I sever from you and that I have I remove from you.

GENITALIA. All that I am I sever from you and that I have I remove from you.

*(***GENITALIA** *removes the ring from* **INTIFADA***'s finger.)*

*(***INTIFADA** *takes* **GENITALIA** *hand in hers.)*

INTIFADA. With this ring I Non-Commit. I remove my hand and heart as I know they will be unsafe with you. All that I am I sever from you and that I have I remove from you.

*(***INTIFADA** *removes the ring from* **GENITALIA***'s finger.)*

OFFICIANT. Genitalia and Intifada, you have given and pledged your promises to each other, and declared your everlasting hatred by removing the rings. Your vows may have been spoken in minutes, but your promises to each other will last until your last breath. Genitalia and Intifada, you have pledged to meet sorrow and happiness as Two Separate Families before God and this community of friends.

(Silence.)

I now pronounce you Ex and Ex-Lax. You may now bitch slap each other.

(They proceed to bitch slap each other.)

Scene Nine. The Last Gay Play

*(**SUTTER** and **LARRY**, sit at a table sipping cocktails, kee-keeing.)*

(A New York Times is on the table between them.)

*(**CLINT** sits at a table near them, also having a drink.)*

LARRY. So what happened?

SUTTER. After I spoke to you?

LARRY. No after you spoke to the Pope – of course after you spoke to me – what happened?

SUTTER. *(coy)*

Well, he came over.

LARRY. Wait – go back.

SUTTER. What?

LARRY. Go to the part where you met him.

SUTTER. I told you he answered my Ad –

LARRY. You have an Ad?

SUTTER. Yeah. So do you.

(Silence.)

LARRY. First of all. I never invite TRADE immediately over to my house. First we meet. Somewhere in public –

SUTTER. So an-ti-way! He came over –

*(**CLINT** turns to **LARRY** and **SUTTER**.)*

CLINT. I'm sorry I was just wondering…

*(He turns to **SUTTER**.)*

Your voice is weird. It's rather…feminine.

SUTTER. Excuse me?

CLINT. Are you gay?

SUTTER. No…

(a la Grey Poupon commercial)

But I do have a taste for Dick every now and then.

(Silence.)

(**LARRY** *tries not to laugh.*)

CLINT. So you're gay?

SUTTER. We're having a conversation here, I don't think –

CLINT. Would you mind if I joined you?

SUTTER. Are you drunk?

CLINT. Yeah.

(**SUTTER** *looks to* **LARRY**.)

(**LARRY** *makes a slight negative gesture.*)

(**SUTTER** *smiles.*)

SUTTER. You can join us. But you have to play nice. No rude comments or I'm going to have to ask you to leave.

CLINT. Fine.

(**CLINT** *pulls his chair up to* **LARRY** *and* **SUTTER**'*s table.*)

I'm Clint.

LARRY. Larry.

SUTTER. Sutter.

CLINT. Do you guys wanna buy me a drink.

SUTTER. No.

CLINT. Okay. I'll be back.

(**CLINT** *exits off to the bar.*)

LARRY. What are you doing?

SUTTER. I'm gonna have a little fun.

LARRY. I don't think we should.

SUTTER. He interrupted our conversation he was rude and I want to play with him for a bit.

LARRY. I just don't think this is going to turn out –

SUTTER. I'm not gonna attack the guy.

LARRY. Okay fine, but if it gets outta hand, I'm leaving.

SUTTER. If it gets outta hand, I'll leave too.

LARRY. I think he's crazy.

SUTTER. I think he's a straight drunk looking for attention.

LARRY. One drink. And then we leave.

SUTTER. Fine with me.

*(**CLINT**, with drink, returns to the table and sits.)*

CLINT. *(blasted)*
So you guys wanna play Truth or Dare?

SUTTER. …Okay.

LARRY. I don't think I wanna play.

SUTTER. He'll play.

CLINT. Great. I'll go first.

SUTTER. Wait a second. Wasn't there a woman sitting with you?

CLINT. Yes.

SUTTER. Is she your girlfriend?

CLINT. No. I met her online.

*(**SUTTER** and **LARRY** exchange looks.)*

SUTTER. Why did she leave?

CLINT. I told her I wanted to fuck her. Truth or Dare?

SUTTER. Truth.

CLINT. What was the last thing you had up your ass?

SUTTER. A cock.

CLINT. Not a dildo?

SUTTER. No.

CLINT. Not a finger?

SUTTER. No.

CLINT. How big was the cock?

SUTTER. Isn't it my turn?

CLINT. Okay.

SUTTER. *(to **CLINT**)*
Truth or Dare.

CLINT. DARE.

SUTTER. Pull your dick out and put it on the table right now.

(Without a moments hesitation, **CLINT** *stands and pulls his cock out and places it on the table in front of* **SUTTER** *and* **LARRY**.*)*

LARRY. *(quick)*
I'm leaving.

SUTTER. Wait.

LARRY. I'm going.

CLINT. *(putting his cock back in his pants)*
Truth or Dare.

SUTTER. *(to* **LARRY***)*
Don't go.

LARRY. Don't dare him again.

CLINT. Truth or Dare.

SUTTER. Truth.

CLINT. What is the biggest dick you've had in your ass?

SUTTER. I don't know. Truth or Dare.

CLINT. Dare.

LARRY. Don't.

CLINT. Dare.

LARRY. Do. Not.

SUTTER. *(excited)*
Kiss my friend, Larry.

*(***CLINT** *kisses* **LARRY**.*)*

*(***LARRY** *is stunned.)*

CLINT. *(to* **LARRY***)*
Truth or Dare.

LARRY. …

SUTTER. Larry.

LARRY. …Truth.

CLINT. How big is your dick?

LARRY. 9 inches.

SUTTER. What!!

LARRY. *(non-chalant)* My girlfriend in High School measured it once.

CLINT. You had a girlfriend?

LARRY. Long time ago.

SUTTER. You have a 9 inch Cock??

LARRY. Yes.

(to **CLINT***)*

Truth or Dare.

CLINT. Truth.

LARRY. Thank god. Okay. Um... Have you ever had sex with a guy?

CLINT. Yes. Truth or Dare.

SUTTER. I still can't believe you have a 9 inch Cock.

LARRY. Get over it.

CLINT. Truth or Dare.

SUTTER. Truth.

CLINT. You guys wanna come back to my Hotel?

(Blackout.)

*(***LARRY** *and* **SUTTER** *sit at table and have had several additional drinks.* **CLINT** *is not there.)*

LARRY. Do you have any idea what time it is?

SUTTER. When are we going to have another opportunity like this one?

LARRY. Sutter, the guy is around the corner buying extra large condoms.

SUTTER. I don't think he'll come back.

LARRY. He took his dick out and placed it on our table, he'll come back!

SUTTER. I think he's lying.

LARRY. I'm not FUCKING HIM!

SUTTER. Larry calm down, we won't even get that far. We'll walk him to his hotel... IF he's actually staying in a Hotel which I doubt. And we'll see what type of excuses he makes up to get out of it.

LARRY. What if he doesn't make up an excuse!

SUTTER. What's the worse thing that could happen? We'll get to his hotel, he'll make an excuse OR he'll call OUR bluff.

LARRY. Thats cruel.

SUTTER. What's cruel about it? He's the one that asked us back to his hotel. You act like he's a 14 year old girl. He's a grown man.

LARRY. It's still cruel.

SUTTER. Fuck that.

LARRY. Sutter.

SUTTER. *(serious)*

Fuck that Larry, I want to Humiliate him.

LARRY. …Why?

SUTTER. *(deadly)*

Because I can.

LARRY. What are you talking about?

SUTTER. You know what I'm talking about… Just for the fun of it.

LARRY. For the fun of what?

SUTTER. He's drunk.

LARRY. You're drunk.

SUTTER. He's corny and horny. He's staying at a Best Western. In Brooklyn. It's perfect.

LARRY. What are you saying?

SUTTER. You know what I'm saying. You knew what I was saying when I began to say it so stop asking me "what am I saying" instead ask your self why the fuck are you still here?

(Silence.)

(whisper)

I can't do this by myself.

LARRY. I'm not –

SUTTER. You just have to hold him down. I'll do the rest.

*(**CLINT** returns with condoms and beer. He's Sloppy Now.)*

(**LARRY** *turns to* **CLINT**.)

LARRY. Why do you want to do this?

CLINT. It'll be fun.

LARRY. You're not gay?

CLINT. Nope.

LARRY. But you want to get fucked?

CLINT. Yep.

LARRY. Why?

CLINT. Because I want to be humiliated.

(**LARRY** *turns to* **SUTTER**. **SUTTER** *smiles.*)

(Blackout.)

(**LARRY**, **SUTTER** *and* **CLINT** *at hotel.*)

(**CLINT** *holds a key card in his hands.*)

CLINT. *(pausing)*
...Wait.

SUTTER. I knew you were bullshit.

CLINT. You have to give me a moment to clean up my room. I haven't had maid service for about 2 weeks.

LARRY. How long have you been here?

CLINT. 2 weeks.

(Beat.)

SUTTER. I want to see what it looks like... Before you clean it up.

LARRY. Why?

CLINT. Why?

SUTTER. Because I think you're bullshit.

CLINT. Okay.

(**CLINT** *swipes his card.*)

(A sound of a door opening is heard.)

SUTTER. *(astonished)*
Okay. We'll wait out here.

(**CLINT** *exits.*)

(Lights shift.)

LARRY. *(quiet)*

What the fuck?

SUTTER. *(quiet)*

That was disgusting.

LARRY. I told you he was crazy.

SUTTER. He is demented.

LARRY. There was shit and blood on that towel on the floor.

SUTTER. You saw shit?

LARRY. And blood. I'm not kidding.

SUTTER. Did you see the peanut butter jar?

LARRY. With the Metro Card in it?

SUTTER. He's been using a Metro Card to eat peanut butter.

LARRY. And the dildos?

SUTTER. That big black one?

LARRY. Yeah. And the BED!

SUTTER. Shhhhh someone might hear us.

LARRY. We should leave.

(**CLINT** *enters completely naked except for a hotel blanket draped on his shoulders.*)

(Silence.)

CLINT. What's wrong?... You guys don't want to do it anymore? If you guys didn't want to do it then why did you guys come back here?

LARRY. You know what? We're really sorry but we can't do this.

CLINT. *(broken)*

Then why did you come? Why didn't you just say no and tell me to get lost?

LARRY. We thought you were kidding.

CLINT. After I put my dick on the table you thought I was kidding?

(Beat.)

SUTTER. …Yes.

CLINT. You know how embarrassing this is for me? I went online to try to meet someone… Just to have a good time. She didn't want to have anything to do with me when I said what I honestly felt.

SUTTER. Clint –

CLINT. I just wanted to have fun with you guys!!

(Silence.)

SUTTER. We're sorry.

CLINT. Thats not good enough!! I'm not some fucking toy you can play around with and lead on and then decide you don't – I have feelings you know. I'm standing here naked in front of two strangers hoping to have a little experience –

SUTTER. We didn't think –

CLINT. I just want to get FUCKED!

(Silence.)

I just want to be held. And Fucked.

(Silence.)

SUTTER. Clint… Can I ask you a serious question?

CLINT. Will you hold me?

SUTTER. Clint.

CLINT. Please. I just want to feel Human. Contact. Just for a moment. Touch me.

*(**SUTTER** looks to **LARRY**.)*

*(**LARRY** nods to **SUTTER** to go to **CLINT**.)*

*(**CLINT** slowly approaches **SUTTER**, who takes him in his arms.)*

(honest)

I repulse a lot of people I know that. I drink too much I laugh too loud I smell funny My eyes are too far apart I'm pigeon toed. And I have nasty thoughts…

SUTTER. *(quiet)*
Clint. Are you on any medication?

CLINT. They make me sleep…

LARRY. Maybe you should take them… Until you… Get to a better place…

CLINT. I don't want to leave my room. Don't wanna go to work. Sometimes I don't even feel like getting up and going to the bathroom… I like pain sometimes… That's why… that's why I asked you guys back here… for some pleasure…pain.

(Silence.)

(Blackout.)

*(**LARRY** and **SUTTER** sit having drinks.)*

*(**LARRY** reads The New York Times that has been sitting at the table throughout.)*

SUTTER. *(referring to New York Times)*
I don't think that was him.

LARRY. It was him. I can't believe we did that.

SUTTER. He wanted us to –

LARRY. We did it.

SUTTER. We didn't do anything. Nothing was done.

LARRY. What about the Desk Clerk at the Best Western?

SUTTER. There wasn't a Desk Clerk at the Best Western.

LARRY. He was sleeping.

SUTTER. There wasn't a Desk Clerk. It was 4am. Clint had a Key Card for the front door and to his Hotel Room.

LARRY. When we were leaving –

SUTTER. What?

LARRY. When we were leaving there was a Desk Clerk sleeping…

SUTTER. There wasn't a fucking –

LARRY. I think he smiled at me…

SUTTER. I thought you said he was sleeping.

LARRY. I think he might have smiled at me though. Like he knew we had just come from having a good time with one of the guests.

SUTTER. So what.

LARRY. They're going to catch us.

SUTTER. No they are not.

LARRY. Every place has cameras.

SUTTER. Listen to me –

LARRY. And we're back at the same fucking place where we met him. This was a stupid idea…

SUTTER. This was the ONLY idea… We don't change our routine. You know how many fucking guys come to this city every day and go to bars every night and go back to their fucking hotel rooms with strangers…

LARRY. No I don't know, how many Sutter??

SUTTER. Lots!

(Silence.)

LARRY. I don't know who you are anymore.

SUTTER. I'm the guy who watched you hold a man down while we raped him with a big black dildo. Remember me now?

(Silence.)

LARRY. I could go to them and tell them it was your idea.

SUTTER. I'm smaller and younger than you.

LARRY. He killed himself because of what we did to him.

SUTTER. No, he walked up to that roof and jumped into traffic because he was off his medicine.

LARRY. A guy died. We had something to do with it and you feel no fucking REMORSE!

SUTTER. Did we beat him with bricks? Did we impale him on a fucking fence??! Did we attach him to our fucking car and drag him through the fucking streets? Did we?! You think those fuckers feel any remorse –

LARRY. I don't want to become Them.

SUTTER. It felt good didn't it? To get back at one of them. It felt good.

LARRY. No.

SUTTER. Truth or Dare.

LARRY. Fuck you.

SUTTER. Truth or Dare.

LARRY. …

SUTTER. TRUTH or –

LARRY. Dare!

(Silence.)

(They look to each other.)

SUTTER. I dare you to go to the Police right now and tell them everything.

(Silence.)

*(**LARRY** starts to leave. Then comes back.)*

LARRY. *(suffer)*

This will haunt me for the rest of my life.

SUTTER. I'm sorry –

LARRY. Don't call me ever again. Don't write me another Email or Text or Speak to me even if you see me begging in the fucking streets.

SUTTER. We didn't kill him Larry.

LARRY. Truth or Dare.

SUTTER. Truth.

(Silence.)

LARRY. You've done this before…

*(**SUTTER** looks at him.)*

*(**LARRY** exits.)*

*(**SUTTER** sits.)*

(Silence.)

*(***ACTOR 4/LARRY** *re-enters abruptly and out of character. He adlibs his frustration over the scene and it brings the other* **ACTORS** *to the Stage from various entrances.)*

(They are dressed in Correctional Outfits.)

ACTOR 5. I don't understand this uh – you have in the scene Sutter holding Clint in his arms, rubbing him like a baby and then they take him into the room and rape him?...

SUTTER. I'm not quite sure about that.

ACTOR 4. The scene goes too far. It's false and gratuitous.

ACTOR 1. *(English accent)* It feels like you want to play the Victim.

SUTTER. Excuse me.

ACTOR 3. *(English accent)* We've been investing in this because we were under the impression that this was based on Real Events...

SUTTER. It's not.

ACTOR 4. So what is the Fucking Audience suppose to think??

SUTTER. I don't wanna do your acting...job...for you.

(The **ACTORS** *look to each other.)*

ACTOR 1. *(English)*

Why did you hire us?

ACTOR 3. *(English)*

Do you think we're Black?

SUTTER. You... You are black.

ACTOR 1. *(English)*

We're putting on those accents you understand...

ACTOR 3. *(English)*

We're not Negroes.

ACTOR 4. *(offended)*

What???

ACTOR 1. *(English)*

We're English.

SUTTER. …I think you should just –

ACTOR 5. You are truly fucked up, and just because some man followed you home from the library and eventually fucked you when you were 16, and you've experienced unrequited love, doesn't mean that you need to rape a mentally unstable person with a big black dildo… And kill him.

ACTOR 1. *(English accent)* This has all been some sick Fantasy of yours.

ACTOR 3. *(English accent)* So why do you need ACTORS???

ACTORS. Exactly!!!

(Silence.)

*(**SUTTER** looks to the **ACTUAL STAGE MANAGER**'s Booth.)*

SUTTER. I'm sorry I'm uh um I'm sorry "*(**STAGE MANAGER**'s Actual Name)*". Could we um…

ACTUAL STAGE MANAGER. Hold please.

*(**SUTTER** is silent. He looks at the audience. He becomes emotional…he stifles himself.)*

*(The **ACTORS** break character further and become their real selves….)*

*(Eventually the **ACTOR** playing **SUTTER** looks at the **STAGE MANAGER**'s Booth.)*

SUTTER. I need my Grandmother.

*(Silence. The Cast look to **SUTTER**.)*

SUTTER. *(quietly to **ACTOR 4**)*

Could I have my Grandmother please.

(Beat.)

ACTUAL STAGE MANAGER. Okay everyone we're going to skip the Prison. And go directly into IPHONE.

*(The stage becomes a machine as we hear the **ACTUAL STAGE MANAGER** calling for the requirements of the scene change.)*

(Everyone involved in the production of this play begins to set the next scene.)

(Sets, lights, costumes.)

(Everything needed for the next scene is done right in front of the audience.)

(We hear the **ACTUAL STAGE MANAGER** *calling the cues to get us into the next scene ending with)*

...Go.

Scene Eleven. IPHONE

(A nursing home.)

(An **OLD GRANNY** *sits in a motorized wheel chair.)*

(She can't move her left arm because of a stroke.)

(Her adult grandson, **SUTTER** *enters.)*

SUTTER. Hi Granny.

*(***OLD GRANNY** *looks away.)*

SUTTER. ...What's wrong Granny?

OLD GRANNY. Who you?

SUTTER. ...You don't recognize me Granny?

*(***OLD GRANNY** *looks at him and then away again.)*

OLD GRANNY. Who you?

SUTTER. I'm your Grandson, Granny. Sutter Boy.

OLD GRANNY. ...I don't know you.

*(***SUTTER** *takes out $20 and holds it out to* **GRANNY***.)*

SUTTER. Here Granny.

*(***OLD GRANNY** *turns and sees the $20.)*

OLD GRANNY. *(reaching for the bill with good arm)* Hey baby, how you doin'?

SUTTER. I'm doing alright. How you doing?

OLD GRANNY. These folks in here don't wanna feed nobody nothing.

SUTTER. They haven't been feeding you?

OLD GRANNY. Nawl, they take some gatdamn cord and put in my belly and tell me that that's feeding me. How you gone feed me with a cord in my belly. I need food in my mouth.

SUTTER. Mama said that the Doctor told you you can't eat solid food anymore. You been having a hard time swallowing.

OLD GRANNY. Fuck that Doctor. I wants me some Ribs and some gatdamn Macaroni and Cheese and some –

SUTTER. Granny you can't have any of that anymore.

OLD GRANNY. Why not?

SUTTER. Because Mama said the Doctor said –

OLD GRANNY. Yo' Mama don't know what the fuck she talkin' about that gatdamn Doctor ain't say no kinda shit like that.

SUTTER. Well you can't have Ribs. You might choke to death.

OLD GRANNY. I been eating Ribs fo' goin' on 85 gatdamn years and I ain't choked to death on nothin' why all of sudden I can't have no food in my mouth? How much sense that make?

SUTTER. I know.

OLD GRANNY. Run down there and pick me up some of 'em Baby Backs.

SUTTER. Granny. Thats not going to happen.

(Silence.)

*(***OLD GRANNY** *looks away.)*

OLD GRANNY. Who you?

SUTTER. Oh now we're back to Alzheimer's? After you done took my $20.

OLD GRANNY. It was suppose to be a FIFTY.

SUTTER. What you gone do with $50 in a Nursing home?

OLD GRANNY. Whatever the fuck I like.

SUTTER. You wanna lose it on Bingo Thursdays.

OLD GRANNY. I ain't never lost no gatdamn $50 at no Bingo been goin' to Bingo for near bout 65 years and I ain't never lost no gatdamn FIFTY.

SUTTER. I brought you something.

OLD GRANNY. Ribs?

SUTTER. No not Ribs Granny. Memories.

OLD GRANNY. Do them Memories come with Barbecue Sauce on 'em? If not, "Who you?"

(Silence.)

*(**SUTTER** takes out an iPhone.)*

What that do?

SUTTER. Lots. You remember how I use to record you and Granddaddy Cussin' and Fussin' all the time.

OLD GRANNY. I don't fuckin' cuss.

(Silence.)

SUTTER. I thought I lost all those old tapes... I used to record you all the time. Especially when you were yellin' at me about something. I put them in Storage a while ago and forgot about them...but then... I realized... I could get them digitized...took me a few months but... Listen.

(He pushes his iPhone.)

*(Lights shift on **OLD GRANNY**.)*

OLD GRANNY. "You laugh like a Grown Gross Gray Ass Frog."

(He pushes.)

"Your voice Rings all through me like a Bell Clapper on a Goose's Ass"

(He pushes.)

"Sit yo' ass down and stop skippin' cross this gatdamn flo'. Don't you hear that gatdamn thunder and lightin'??!!!"

(Lights shift back.)

Where the hell did you get those from?

SUTTER. I told you I recorded them when I was little.

OLD GRANNY. Why on earth would you ever record some shit like that?

SUTTER. Because I loved the way you spoke.

OLD GRANNY. The way I spoke? I spoke like a human person.

SUTTER. No Granny. You spoke a little different.

OLD GRANNY. I spoke like everybody else spoke –

(He pushes.)

(Lights shift.)

"I can't even wipe my ass without somebody callin' my GATdamn name!"

(Lights shift back.)

SUTTER. I got conversations. Like you and Mama.

(He pushes.)

(Lights shift.)

*(***MIDDLE AGED MOTHER*** appears in a wedding dress.)*

OLD GRANNY. *(to* **YOUNG MOTHER***)*
What the fuck you gon' put on a White Dress fo'?

MIDDLE AGED MOTHER. What's wrong with this white dress?

OLD GRANNY. What's wrong with it?

MIDDLE AGED MOTHER. Yeah what's wrong with it Mama?

OLD GRANNY. Ask them two gatdamn kids you already gat from two different baby daddies what's wrong with it?

MIDDLE AGED MOTHER. That don't mean nothing. That's old fashion to think you can't wear a white dress just because you have kids.

OLD GRANNY. By two different baby daddies.

MIDDLE AGED MOTHER. You had twelve gatdamn kids Mama!

OLD GRANNY. And they all gat the SAME GATdamn BABY DADDY.

MIDDLE AGED MOTHER. Well I'm wearing this WHITE Dress at my Wedding.

OLD GRANNY. Then I won't be there.

MIDDLE AGED MOTHER. What?

OLD GRANNY. And you can't have it in my gatdamn church with my gatdamn pastor.

MIDDLE AGED MOTHER. You don't run that Church.

OLD GRANNY. You ain't gon' be struttin' down no gatdamn aisle of MY church in a white gatdamn dress with two gatdamn kids from two different baby daddies carryin' rings behind you.

MIDDLE AGED MOTHER. This is my wedding day Mama. Not yours!

*(**MIDDLE AGED MOTHER** stomps out.)*

(Lights shift back.)

SUTTER. Mama cried all that night.

OLD GRANNY. She got married tho' didn't she?

SUTTER. Yes ma'am.

OLD GRANNY. In my Church?

SUTTER. Yes ma'am.

OLD GRANNY. Was I there?

SUTTER. Yes you were there Granny.

OLD GRANNY. Is she happy?

(Silence.)

SUTTER. Yes. I think she's happy Granny.

OLD GRANNY. Then that's all that matters.

(Silence.)

(He drops the iPhone by mistake.)

(Lights shift.)

*(A **WHITE MAN** appears.)*

May I help you Sir?

WHITE MAN. Yes I'm looking for a young man, named Sutter.

OLD GRANNY. That's my Grandson, how may I help you Sir?

WHITE MAN. He's friends with my son, Roy.

OLD GRANNY. Ok.

WHITE MAN. I saw Sutter the other day and I just wanted to make sure he was alright.

OLD GRANNY. Is somethin' the matter Sir.

WHITE MAN. No ma'am. I just wanted to make sure that… that he was okay.

OLD GRANNY. Why wouldn't he be okay?

(to offstage)

Sutter Boy!!

*(**SUTTER** speaks in the opposite direction of **OLD GRANNY**.)*

SUTTER. *(laughing to offstage)*

Ma'am??

OLD GRANNY. *(to offstage)*

Come out heah!

*(**SUTTER**, becomes a **TEENAGER**…)*

SUTTER. *(still laughing to **OLD GRANNY**)*

Ma'am?

*(**SUTTER** notices the **WHITE MAN**.)*

(They stare at each other for long moment.)

(A secret is shared between them.)

OLD GRANNY. You know this man, Sutter boy?

SUTTER. Yes ma'am.

OLD GRANNY. Somethin' happen that he need to be comin' here to make sure you alright?

SUTTER. Yes ma'am.

OLD GRANNY. …Is you alright?

SUTTER. …I'm alright.

*(**OLD GRANNY** looks to **WHITE MAN** who has not stopped looking at **SUTTER**.)*

WHITE MAN. …Good…

OLD GRANNY. How do you know my Sutter Boy, Sir?

WHITE MAN. Oh…we met at the Library.

(beat)

And he knows my son, Roy.

(Silence.)

*(***WHITE MAN*** disappears.)*

(Lights shift back.)

OLD GRANNY. Is that suppose to mean somethin' to me?

SUTTER. ...No ma'am... It means something to me... I must have left the tape recorder on...sometimes I'd hide it in the hallway...then listen to what it recorded later at night...

OLD GRANNY. There is really somethin' wrong with you boy.

SUTTER. That's not the one I wanted you to hear. This is the one.

OLD GRANNY. Is you gonna run on down there and –

*(***SUTTER*** pushes.)*

(Lights shift.)

*(***YOUNG BLACK MOM*** appears.)*

*(***SUTTER*** is now young.)*

Do that move Michael Jackson lak ta do.

*(***SUTTER*** does some old skool MJ moves.)*

*(***YOUNG BLACK MOM*** watches.)*

(clapping)

Get it... Get it... Get it... Get it...

YOUNG BLACK MOM. That's all he like to do. Dance and read that Dictionary I bought him.

OLD GRANNY. Ain't nuthin' wrong with dat... You wait till he start runnin' behind these little girls you better hope he just want to dance and read some dictionary book 'stead of gettin' one of 'em fast tail heifas pregnant...

YOUNG BLACK MOM. I ain't raisin' nobody's babies.

OLD GRANNY. That's exactly what I said before you had this one and look how many times you dropping him off over here for the weekENDS that turns into the week BEGINS.

YOUNG BLACK MOM. I need a break sometimes.

OLD GRANNY. And I don't need no gatdamn break?? I was just suppose to raise my twelve gatdamn kids and THEY kids too????...

YOUNG BLACK MOM. Mama you know you like to have them runnin' all over the place.

OLD GRANNY. What the hell makes you think that?

YOUNG BLACK MOM. Cuz you let 'em.

OLD GRANNY. I let 'em cuz I don't want them out there in them streets like you and yo' gatdamn hard headed brothers and sisters...all ya'll know how to do was eat, shit and run the streets.

*(**SUTTER** stops doin MJ moves and catches his breath but speaks anyway.)*

SUTTER. Granny –

YOUNG BLACK MOM. Don't you hear me and Mama talkin'? I don' told you about interruptin' grown people's conversation.

SUTTER. But I got a question about my Booty Candy.

OLD GRANNY. What???

YOUNG BLACK MOM. *(to* **SUTTER***)*

Shut up and go sit down somewhere.

OLD GRANNY. Wait a second –

YOUNG BLACK MOM. Mama don't –

OLD GRANNY. What he wanna know about a Booty Candy fo'?

YOUNG BLACK MOM. I don't know what he wanna know he been talkin' about it for the last week, he got some letter from that little mannish girl, Alessa, next door to me, need her ass beat.

OLD GRANNY. What you wanna know about Booty Candies fo' Sutter?

YOUNG BLACK MOM. Mama I said –

OLD GRANNY. You member to pull yourself back and wash?

YOUNG BLACK MOM. Gatdammit. Here we go.

SUTTER. I always remember to pull myself back and wash, but Granny, Mama said if I forget to do it, then my Booty Candy would fall off.

(Silence.)

*(**OLD GRANNY** looks to **YOUNG BLACK MOM**.)*

OLD GRANNY. You told this boy his Dick would fall off?

SUTTER. Mama say you ain't suppose to say "Dick," Granny.

OLD GRANNY. That's a damn shame.

*(to **SUTTER**)*

Your Bootycandy will Not fall off, Sutter.

SUTTER. That's what I thought. Mama said you ain't suppose to lick it or let nobody else lick it.

*(**OLD GRANNY** looks to **YOUNG BLACK MOM**.)*

YOUNG BLACK MOM. You started it. Gone finish it.

OLD GRANNY. *(to **SUTTER**)*

You ain't suppose to lick it Sutter. But… When you get older… Some folks lak to have it licked…

SUTTER. Like them folks in them magazines that Uncle Terry and Uncle Alphonso have under the bathtub upstairs?

(Silence.)

*(**OLD GRANNY** looks to **YOUNG BLACK MOM**, who smiles broadly.)*

YOUNG BLACK MOM. *(to **OLD GRANNY**, mocking)*

"Get it… Get it… Get it…"

*(**YOUNG BLACK MOM** disappears.)*

SUTTER. Why them BootyCandies so BIG!! Is that what happens when they get happy from the Lickin'!!??? And Granny, I got a idea about somethin'… I think that if Boys was just allowed to lick other Boys' BootyCandies, there would be peace in the world cuz then they wouldn't be mad at each other and start tryin' to kill each other cuz they BootyCandies would be happy and they would grow Big from the lickin' and they could play BootyCandy games instead of making wars and stuff.

(Dead silence.)

(Lights shift back.)

OLD GRANNY. You have lost your mind in Real Life.

(Silence.)

SUTTER. When was the last time you had Ribs Granny?...

OLD GRANNY. I can't remember, why?

SUTTER. You really want some?

OLD GRANNY. No. I really want some mo' of that Tofu pumped into my gatdamn belly.

SUTTER. Okay... We have to be sneaky about this.

OLD GRANNY. I can't be too gatdamn sneaky in this wheelchair.

SUTTER. I'm gonna get you some Ribs but you have to promise not to tell Mama.

OLD GRANNY. What the hell I need to tell your Mama fo'?

SUTTER. Alright.

(He works on his iPhone.)

*(**OLD GRANNY** watches.)*

(After a moment.)

OLD GRANNY. When you leavin to get the Ribs?

SUTTER. I'm doing it now.

OLD GRANNY. The Ribs down the street.

SUTTER. I know.

OLD GRANNY. You trying to tell me that the Ribs gonna come out of that thing you got in your hand?

SUTTER. Yes.

Do you want Short Ribs?

OLD GRANNY. I don't want no gatdamn Short Ribs I want my Baby Backs!

SUTTER. Keep your voice down Granny…this has to be our Secret…

OLD GRANNY. *(whispers secret)*
I want my Baby Backs!!

SUTTER. They got a Baby Backs and Short Ribs Feast…

OLD GRANNY. What the Feast come with…

SUTTER. A half slab of pork ribs and two chunks of beef ribs…

OLD GRANNY. Yeah give me that…

SUTTER. What sides you want?

OLD GRANNY. What they got?

SUTTER. Mashed potatoes.

OLD GRANNY. Yes.

SUTTER. Baked Potatoes

OLD GRANNY. Yes.

SUTTER. Sweet Potato Fries.

OLD GRANNY. That too.

SUTTER. Granny.

OLD GRANNY. Don't Granny me… I'm 85 gatdamn years old. Keep going.

SUTTER. Potato pancakes.

OLD GRANNY. Anything with potato in it. Get it.

SUTTER. Macaroni and Cheese

OLD GRANNY. Now we cookin'.

SUTTER. Baked Beans.

OLD GRANNY. Yes sweet Jesus. With some bacon in em.

SUTTER. Corn on the Cob.

OLD GRANNY. Yes.

SUTTER. Creamed corn.

OLD GRANNY. Yes.

SUTTER. Cut Sweet Corn.

OLD GRANNY. Yes.

SUTTER. Onion Rings.

OLD GRANNY. Mmm-hmm…

SUTTER. Grilled Vegetables.

OLD GRANNY. Fuck I need some grilled Vegetables for?

SUTTER. Steamed Spinach.

OLD GRANNY. It got Bacon in it?

SUTTER. I doubt it. Collard Greens.

OLD GRANNY. BINGO!!!

SUTTER. Shh!! Granny…

OLD GRANNY. Put some bacon in them collards for me baby.

SUTTER. Alright… There… Done.

OLD GRANNY. What we do now?

SUTTER. We wait.

OLD GRANNY. Ain't you gotta call 'em?

SUTTER. No ma'am.

OLD GRANNY. How they gonna know what we want?

SUTTER. I just told them…

OLD GRANNY. Oh…okay.

(Silence.)

You need my $20 back?

SUTTER. No. I already paid for it.

OLD GRANNY. How you do that?

SUTTER. You can do a lot of things with this Granny.

OLD GRANNY. I guess so.

(Silence.)

So now we just wait?

SUTTER. We just wait.

OLD GRANNY. We still gotta be sneaky?

SUTTER. Not as much…

OLD GRANNY. Okay…

(Silence.)

(Silence.)

(Silence.)

Sutter boy.

SUTTER. Yes Granny?

OLD GRANNY. Do that dance that Michael Jackson useta lak to do…

End of Play.

(NOTE ON CURTAIN CALL:)

(It is the playwright's wish that every production use their curtain call as a tribute to the LEGENDARY MICHAEL JACKSON.)

(DANCE!!! DANCE!!! DANCE!!!)